Ultimate Brain Games and Teasers

Creative Mind Games for Smart Kids of All Ages (Ages 5 to 15)

Annabelle Erikson

Table of Contents

Don't forget,
if you like my book,
or even if you don't,
I want to hear about it!
I encouraged you to leave
A review on Amazon.
Help others decide to buy!

Introduction

"The solution often turns out more beautiful than the puzzle," so said Richard Dawkins, a famous biologist and author.

That is true for brain teasers as well. The simple joy of solving the complex puzzle they provide is truly rewarding. Plus, you get to feel extremely smart. Nonetheless, what are brain teasers really?

You have probably encountered brain teasers in your life. You may have seen one at the back of a cereal box for the first time or from a book that your school teacher had suggested once. The good thing about these brain games is that they are timeless and will always keep sharpening your mind.

What Exactly Is a Brain Teaser?

A brain teaser is a type of a puzzle that requires you to think in order to solve it. In many cases, the teasers ask for unconventional and lateral thinking to resolve the games. The latter is a method of solving problems that requires creativity as opposed to more direct mathematical formulas.[1]

One of the earliest personalities known for his love for brainteasers was Archimedes, a Greek Mathematician. He

---

[1] Dashner, J. (2008). *The journal of curious letters.* Washington: Shadow Mountain.

regularly created mathematical puzzles for his colleagues to solve.[2]

The complexity of brainteasers depends on the information that the person has with him or her. This is evident in most puzzles because people's minds largely apply a condition of probability. This means that we, humans, weigh the answers based on the data that we have and choose the one that makes most sense to us. We are so complex aren't we?

One simple example of such a mind teaser is the *Two Children Problem*. Here are a couple of questions that come from this source.

1. Mr. Jones has two children. If the older child is a girl, what is the probability that both are girls?

2. Mr. Smith has two children. If one child is a boy, what is the probability that both are boys?

The answers to questions one and two are ½ and ⅓, respectively. However, the answer to the second question may also be ½, depending on the additional information availed.

The term *"brain teaser"* is often used interchangeably with *"brain puzzles,"* although they are slightly different. The former is a verbal or (in many cases) a written answer in a

---

[2] Gardner, M. (1954). *The second scientific American book of mathematical puzzles and diversions.* New York: Simon & Schuster.

couple of sentences to describe a problem. A great example is a riddle.[3] A *brain puzzle,* on the other hand, is a game that challenges your thinking and logical skills.

Brain Teasers and Cognitive Function

What exactly is cognition? In simple terms, it is the ability by which we interact with the world around us. It is the collection of processes that we humans use to engage with various factors in the environment.

Cognitive abilities are related to the condition of the brain. This is because they help us use the brain to solve problems, make connections, and even pay attention to the elements in our environment.

Brain teasers develop the brain in many ways. They improve perception, which is essential to understand stimuli. That sounds rather complex! But what it essentially means is that brain teasers help your brain to understand your sense. What am I smelling right now? What is this taste in my mouth? What is that beautiful sight I am looking at? All of these elements are understood by the brain.

When you deal with brain teasers, you have to not only understand the problem, but also remember its various parts. And guess what develops by practicing remembering various facts? Your memory of course!

----

[3] Reader's Digest Association. (2007). *Puzzles & brain teasers: Sudoku puzzles, word games, visual challenges, and tests of logic.* Washington: Reader's Digest Association.

Did you also know that brain teasers help us understand language better? How, you ask? Well, you are translating problems into a language that you understand. This further helps you process other languages easily.

So with all of these benefits, it surely looks like everyone should get in on the brain teaser fun!

Well, they should. And many are already challenging themselves to complex brain teasers every day.

Brain teasers are not restricted to a certain type. Even solving Sudoku is a way to tease your brain into developing some impressive abilities. Some of them might almost sound like a superpower.
Think about it. Visual processing? Spatial awareness?

Today, you might be motivated to play these brain teasers either for fun or to test yourself. Nevertheless, they are more than simple mind games as they can help to keep your memory strong and sharp if you practice them regularly.

Did you know that your brain has a feature called neuroplasticity? This means that it will change and shift with time. The brain will age as you grow older, become less powerful, and less competent. By keeping your brain focused on puzzles like brain teasers, you can mold it to remain more active throughout your life. In other words, brain teasers are like batteries; they recharge your mind!

Teasers that challenge the brain's normal thinking process can keep it stimulated, you see. They also help encourage the body to function in various ways and try new activities. By applying lateral thinking, you may even feel fresh and creative.

Using brain teasers with your kids is a great way to assist them in developing problem-solving skills no matter what kind of situation they may be facing. This book was created to help you introduce mind games to children of all ages, which can be beneficial for their early development.

The book has a collection of brain teasers to test the problem-solving capabilities of kids aged between five to 15.

Note: you can check for the correct answers to the questions at the end of the book.

But don't just go straight there. Challenge your brain first!

Chapter 1: All You Need to Know About Brain Teasers

Every medical expert out there may advise you to do things that may enhance your brain health and memory strength. In one of the studies conducted at John Hopkins, researchers in brain functioning demonstrated that it is possible to enhance the brain memory by regularly playing different brain teasers.[4]

This chapter digs deeper into mind games to help you understand what they are for. It explores the core benefits that come with engaging in brain teasers and shows the proper ways to solve them. It also provides useful tips and tricks that you should use when answering the brain games.

Why You Need Some Brain Teasing

It Promotes Active Participation and Student Engagement
To unravel numerous brain teasers, kids can work in small groups or even involve adults. They are immersed in deeper thinking to resolve the problems at hand. This helps them learn to appreciate different activities inside or outside of school (Gardner, 1954).

Some teachers also use brain teasers as warm-ups for students before starting lessons or activities. One or two

---

[4] Price, M. (2017). John Hopkins Researchers say doing this will improve your brain power. Retrieved from http://fortune.com/2017/10/23/johns-hopkins-brain-function/

minutes of mind games can help prepare their minds for the subject at hand. If the teacher is creative enough, he or she can even design the teasers to reflect everyday situations that the kids may experience, adding a little valuable lesson along the way. The teacher can also come up with riddles about the environment, student roles, and community.

When the lesson ends, the schoolteacher can use the mind games to encourage students to engage each other as they brainstorm answers or review the problems. By enabling kids to interact with each other, teachers can effectively aid the learners to prepare for the bigger roles that require teamwork in society later.

It Is a Unique Way of Encouraging Children to Learn

For young kids, learning and growth happen at a very tender point. However, it is never too early to start exploring different subjects and figure out how they work in life. Brain teasers provide kids with challenges that allow them to check out their environment, understand other people, and learn to work with peers. They teach them about animals, leaders, and treasure as well, among others.

The mind games help kids to start thinking positively and learn important concepts such as sharing, caring for animals, and even friendships. For instance, most riddles are created to provide moral lessons that children can easily associate with. This is a great way to start building a responsible person in a society.

It Boosts Memory Power

When you engage in physical training, one of its effects is that it strengthens your physical being. In a similar way, if you train your brain using mind teasers, the activity can strengthen your memory. As you work on different mind games, too, different parts of the brain get engaged to keep the thoughts flowing.

Researchers have revealed that the prefrontal cortex, ventral temporal occipital cortex, and posterior parietal cortex function simultaneously when trying to solve brain teasers (Dashner, 2008). These areas help improve memory. When you strengthen the mind, the additional brain power will manifest even in other areas, such as resolving complex situations.

If you are still in school, brain teasers will make it easy to solve cognitive-related problems. For example, remembering the things you've been taught by tutors or found in books can be effortless for you. Therefore, you can successfully pass your exams and build a good career foundation.

It Increases Brain Processing Speed

One advantage of using brain teasers is being able to get the correct answers to a question within a short timeframe. In many instances, after all, you will only have a few minutes to get the answer right. Hence, it is crucial for your brain to process information fast.

The target is to ensure that you can apply different problem-solving methods to get the right solutions for the brain teasers. In other areas such as home or school, you will also enjoy faster brain processing capacities.

Note: You should train your brain to solve different types of teasers to be able to handle most challenges in life.

It Reduces Boredom

We have all been there! We find ourselves without any activity to help our brains stay focused. Soon, we just end up bored. Through brain teasers, kids can sharpen the brain and increase their productivity, all the while getting rid of their boredom spells!

Brain teasers are reliable options for breaking monotony. If you were learning a specific subject and want to shift to a different one, brain teasers can help you to make the transition smooth. Do not simply jump from one subject to another, sharpen the brain with teasers and prepare it for the next task.[5]

It Provides Emotional Satisfaction

When you are trying to search for answers to brain teasers, it is like a journey with multiple challenges. You feel challenged to get the answers. Therefore, decoding the mind games correctly provides a unique sense of

[5] Argasinski, J. & Wegrzyn, P. (2018). Affective patterns in serious games. *Future Generation Computer Systems, 92*, 526-538. doi: 10.1016/j.future.2018.06.013

emotional satisfaction. You will feel emboldened to take newer and more challenging teasers.[6] For kids, this encourages them to take up big challenges at school or in their lives in general.

If you take brain teasers regularly, unraveling them will help to make kids feel more successful. When the same level of lateral thinking is applied in school, kids can expect an equally high level of satisfaction because of elevated productivity.

It Enhances Kids' Ability to Perform Complex Tasks Under Pressure

In some instances such as when employers ask brain teasers in interviews, the target is not to simply pick the right answers. Rather, they are interested in knowing your ability to perform optimally under stressful conditions. Indeed, they might even be interested in the process as opposed to only focusing on the answer (Argasinski & Wegrzyn, 2019).

Brain teasers prepare you to look at complex issues from multiple angles and solving them correctly (Gardner, 1954). If kids can effectively handle most of the brain teasers, especially the complex ones, the chances are that many tasks at school will be like a walk in the park for them!

---

[6] Moore, G. (2010). *10-minute brain teasers: Brain-training tips, logic tests, and puzzles to exercise your mind*. New York: Skyhorse.

Tip to Solving Brain Teasers

To solve the brain teasers correctly, it is important to prepare yourself for them. You need to delve into the world of creative thinking to get the right answers. Here are the three most important things that you should realize to answer the brain teaser questions well.

Commence With Junior Brain Teasers

Start with simple brain teasers before advancing to the more complex ones.[7] This will help kids' minds to be able to handle bigger challenges that come on the way (Moore, 2010). For example, if you have a young kid, consider advising him/her to start with brain teasers for children aged 5-8 years before moving to the tougher teasers.

When kids begin early, they develop special interest in brain teasers such that most of them become easy to tackle. Remember to get a wide collection of the teasers for the child to get exposed.

Ensure to Get the Right Environment

In many cases, brain teasers require you to use different analytical methods to arrive at the right answers. This will need the right environment. For example, if you need to make some calculations, it is advisable to be in a cool environment devoid of distractions.

---

[7] Vervoort, J. (2019). New frontiers in futures games: leveraging game sector developments. *Futures, 105*, 174-186.

Make Sure to Have the Right Tools

When you are trying to solve a complex brain teaser, you need to make some calculations, eliminate the obvious odd options, and follow the right procedure. It is, therefore, crucial to have tools such as a pen and notebook, your phone, or a computer.

If you are using an online challenge, your computer or tablet need fast internet connectivity to follow specific characters, games, or check for hints. Therefore, the tools for every brain teaser will depend on the nature of the activity and level of complexity. In many cases, you will simply need a pen and paper.

Tips & Tricks

When you answer a brain teaser correctly, it makes you feel good. In addition to the above three steps on solving brain teasers, here are additional ideas to help you get the brain teasers right:

Develop a Passion for Brain Teasers.

This will give you the urge to look for newer challenges and learn how to conquer them with time.

Stay Relaxed When Taking Brain Teasers

When a brain teaser is put forward, being relaxed will help you look at it from different angles.[8]

Do Not Fear to Ask for More Information When You See a Teaser

The information given for a specific teaser determines how easily it can be solved. If you notice that some additional information is needed, do not hesitate to ask for it or check the teaser from a different publication.

Research Complex Brain Teasers

If you find a brain teaser that is too complicated for you, do not get discouraged because you cannot know everything. Take time to explore the teaser and how to handle it. This could be the secret you need to easily solve other complex brain teasers.

Know That the Brain Teaser's Complexity Will Continue to Intensify

If you take brain teasers at lower levels, they are relatively simple to understand and solve. However, the complexity keeps intensifying as the brain teasers advance. Therefore, it is advisable to keep following the complexity continuum to be able to solve more complex brain teasers.

---

[8] Reader's Digest. (2004). *Reader's Digest book of puzzles & brain teasers*. New York: Reader's Digest Association.

Always Explain the Answer for Your Brain Teaser

In some cases, the target for brain teasers is not simply to get an answer. Rather, they are aimed at exploring how to go about solving the question under consideration. Therefore, explaining the method you used to resolve a teaser could get you some points.

There Is No Harm in Making Mistakes

The best part about trying to solve a complex brain teaser is that it is okay to make mistakes. What helps you gain more understanding and develop your brain is the fact that you can learn new ways to approach the problem. Every mistake is a learning experience that boosts creativity and confidence.

Chapter 2: Beginner Games and Teasers (Ages 5 to 8)

If you have a kid, it is important to introduce brain teasers to them early in life. This helps the child to learn how to tackle different challenges anywhere they may be. Most brain teasers for kids between 5 and 8 years old are simple and fun. This chapter explores three different types of mind teasers for this age range: fun wordplay, brain benders, and quick questionnaires.

Each of these brain teasers challenge kids to think of a problem in a different way. With fun wordplay, kids learn to use and improve their language skills to find solutions to answers. With brain benders, kids get to connect the two halves of their brains to create some unique set of skills. Plus, they receive a wholesome brain development. Finally, with quick questionnaire, you encourage kids to understand the world around them. It makes them aware of what surrounds them.

Fun Wordplay

Fun wordplay is meant to allow young kids to enjoy using words and applying them in different situations (Moore, 2010). This teaser may inspire the children to become creative from an early age and prepare them for more complicated things they might encounter once they grow up.

At home, your youngsters can have some fun by checking words that rhyme with each other. For instance, bee-tree, knee-ghee, cat-mat, and sat-rat. This makes the brain teasers as interesting as possible.

The primary goal of fun wordplay is to give children a mind game that they can easily identify with at their age. More importantly, the words need to reflect what the kids experience in their own environment. Here are fun wordplay questions for kids between 5 and 8 years old.

1. Name two words that start with letter "B" and end with letter "Y."
2. How many words can you make out of the letters in "School Bus"? The words must have two or more letters.
3. Give the kids a list of words that they easily recognize or was part of their school curriculum. Then, ask them to pick the word that was spelled incorrectly. Here is an example:

Which of the following words do not have the right spelling? Apple, rabit, dentist, airplane, robot.

4. People purchase me to eat but no one eats me.
5. What can be seen once in a minute, twice in a moment, and never in a thousand years?
6. Think of something that only increases and never decreases.

Special Tip: To get the correct answers with wordplay, it is important to practice with basic words before trying to grow your vocabularies. Besides, ensure to go through more word-based teasers to learn more.

Brain Benders

Brain benders are more complex than wordplay. They are unique types of mind exercises that help kids to practice with both sides of the brain. The left hemisphere helps to recognize letters and process signs, while the right hemisphere assists with arrangement of the letters.[9]

Note that the brain benders will only be helpful if you stimulate the brain and try working them through. In some cases, there can be more than a single answer, too. The following are some great mind benders for you.

1. HOME
2. MEREPEAT
3. Iesur
4. R+O+S=K
5. Class
6. Oddsus
7. Brain
8. HeaRtBeAt
9. HOUDMSE
10. NtUS

Special Tip: Make sure to think broadly about the words. Remember that there can be more than one answer for every question as well.

---

[9] Realizations Inc. (n.d.). Set fifty-six. Retrieved from https://arlenetaylor.org/brain-exercises/brain-benders/549-set-fifty-six

Quick Questionnaire

The brain teasers that involve quick questionnaires are designed to test a child's knowledge on different subjects.[10] To make them more interesting, it is best to classify them based on ages. For example, most questionnaires for young kids revolve around their surroundings and the things that they have learned over time.

The quick questionnaires are aimed at challenging young kids to keep building their knowledge. Unlike the mind benders, though, questionnaires require specific answers. Here are great quick questionnaires for kids aged from 5 to 8 years old (Reader's Digest, 2004).

1. Name one thing that goes up and down but does not move in reality.
2. Where do you find oceans, lakes, and rivers with no water?
3. Name one thing that is always dirty when it is white yet clean when black.
4. Name one word that becomes shorter after adding two letters to it.
5. It has hands but cannot clap.
6. Name one thing that will always get bigger as you keep taking it away.

---

[10] Silverthorne, S. & Warner, J. (2010). *Mind-boggling one-minute mysteries and brain teasers.* New York: Harvest House.

7. Name one thing that travels across the globe but only stays in one corner.
8. Name one item that has a lot of keys but cannot open a door.
9. Name one item that has many holes but can hold water.
10. Identify the item that gets wet when dry.

The questionnaires can also be open to help your kid think broadly. The design of such questions help them direct their focus to a specific area of life. Some examples include business, engineering, medicine, and other niches. Note that there are no distinct answers to these questionnaires.

1. What would you like to be when you grow up?
2. Have you ever thought of renaming the colors of crayons?
3. If you had to have a superpower, what would it be?
4. Name the things that make you feel brave.
5. If you want to write a book, what will it be about?
6. If you could open a shop, what items would your shop have?
7. If you were asked to give your family members new names, what would they be?

Chapter 3: Intermediate Games and Teasers (Ages 9 to 12)

For intermediate children, the brain teasers seek to provoke logical thinking and problem-solving capabilities at an early stage. As their school subjects and understanding of the environment broaden, these kids should be able to tackle more challenges compared to the younger kids below the age of 8.

This chapter explores arithmetic activities that largely involve numbers, puzzles, and mysteries that are ideal for kids between 9 and 12 years old.

Arithmetic Activities

In this collection, there are tricky and engaging math activities to challenge your elementary child's mind. One of the important factors about math is that it helps develop a child's critical thinking skills. Math is all about logic and order. Every problem requires you to follow a certain number of steps before you can reach the conclusion. When a child engages in the process of finding these steps, two things happen. First, the process involved in trying to figure out the problem and finding a logical solution gives their brain a workout! This enhances their problem solving skills. Second, trying to figure out the steps takes time. As kids go from one phase to another, they learn to be disciplined and focused. What this does is improve a kid's attention, memory, and their ability to notice details.

1. A granddad, 2 dads, and 2 sons went to a movie theater and purchased a ticket for each. What is the total number of tickets that they purchased?

2. If you add the ages of a father and a son, the total comes to 66. However, the father's age is the age of the son reversed. How old can they be?

3. A duck was offered $9, a bee $27, and a spider $36. Depending on this information, how much would a cat get?

4. There is a number that is odd. However, if you remove a letter, it becomes even. What number is that?

5. A little girl goes shopping in the market and buys 12 tomatoes. When going home, all the tomatoes except 9 get ruined. How many tomatoes did the girl manage to take home?

6. Allen had $28.75 in his pocket. Then, he purchased three cookies at $1.5 each, five magazines at $0.5 each, and five flowers at $1.25 each. The rest was used to buy sunglasses. What was the cost of the sunglasses?

7. What weighs more, a pound of stone or a pound of feathers?

8. Four carpenters can build four tables in 4 hours. How many tables can be built by eight men in 8 hours?

9. Mary, Jane, and Rose went to have a cup of coffee at a restaurant. The total bill was $12, and they agreed to split it equally. If Jane paid $4 and Rose paid $4 too, who paid the remaining bill?

10. If you have a rooster that lays two eggs every day for breakfast, how many eggs will you have in two weeks?

Puzzling Puzzles

These puzzles describe unusual scenarios and require you to try and establish what is happening to get the correct answers.[11] Puzzles allow the child to think outside the box. This further enhances their creative abilities. When they begin to use their imagination to figure out a problem, they automatically begin to train their minds to use more creative ways to reach a solution.

1. If a blue house is made of blue bricks and a pink house is made of pink bricks, what color of bricks is a greenhouse made of?

2. Your only ping-pong ball has fallen into a metal pipe that is fixed about one foot deep into a block of concrete. What is the best way to get the ball out if you only have shoelaces, a tennis paddle, and a plastic water bottle?

3. How can you throw a ball so hard and have it get back to you without bouncing off anything? There is no one who throws the ball back, and it is not attached to anything.

4. You are in a room with only two metal rods. One of them is a magnet. How can you identify which metal is the magnet?

5. It was a snowy Christmas, and a family of four was getting ready for dinner. The father was reading the newspaper, the youngest son was doing his homework, the eldest son was mowing the lawn, and

[11] Riddles. (2017). Math riddles. Retrieved from https://www.getriddles.com/math-riddles/

the mother was watching TV. When the family entered the living room, they found out that someone had eaten all the food! Who ate all their Christmas food?

6. One philosopher forgot to wind up his favorite clock in his living room. He did not have a radio, internet, television or other means of knowing time. Then, he traveled to his friend's place several miles into the desert. He stayed at his friend's house for sometime and then came back. However, he correctly reset the clock. How did he know the time?

7. Four angels were sitting on a Christmas tree among other beautiful ornaments. Two of the angels had blue halos, while the other two had yellow. However, none of them was able to see above their head.

Angel "A" was sitting on top of a branch and could easily see angels "C" and "B" who sat below him. Angel "B" was able to see angel "C" who was also placed underneath. Angel "D" was at the bottom of the tree, however, where he was hidden by thick branches. Therefore, no angel could see him, and he could not see any of them either.
Which angel could be the first to guess their own color and shout for others to hear?

8. A lady who lives on the 10th floor takes an elevator down to the first floor when going to work. In the evening when there are people on the elevator or during rainy days, she goes straight to her floor using the elevator. In other days, she takes the elevator to the 7th floor and uses the stairs to reach her apartment. Can you explain the reason for it?

9. In a one-story blue house, there was a blue person, a blue cat, a blue fish, a blue computer, a blue chair, a blue table, a blue telephone, and a blue door – everything was blue! What color were the stairs?

Mind-Boggling Mysteries

These teasers are meant to help you think outside the box as you search for answers and juggle multiple scenarios.

1. There is a man who is looking at a clock that shows the correct time. But he still does not know what time it is. Why is that? (CLUES BELOW)
    - The man can see and tell time well, so there is no chance that he cannot recognize the time.
    - The clock is normal and the man can see it clearly. There is nothing blocking the clock.
    - There is more than one clock in the room.

2. During the time of the old West, a cowboy rides into town on Sunday. He stays for three days, and leaves on Sunday. How can this be?

3. A man walks into a room with only one match. He notices that he has to light a lantern, a gas stove, the pilot light of a water heater and a fire in a fireplace. He can only light one item in the room. Which one should he light first?

4. Mary tells John, "I found a ten-dollar bill between the pages 15 and 16 of my storybook. Do you want it?" However, John refuses by saying, "You did not find any ten-dollar bill at all!" How did he know that?

5. Jack told Mark, "Imagine that you was in a room with no doors, no windows, and no other ways of escaping. The room was slowly filling with water. How do you escape?" Mark replied, "That's easy. I already know

the answer." How did Mark find a way to escape the room?

6. There was a man who was taking a walk outside. Suddenly, it started to rain heavily. As the man did not have an umbrella, his clothes were completely wet. However, not a single hair on his head got wet. What is it so?

7. A man was sitting at home when a snowball struck his window. Upon opening the window and looking out, he noticed three boys running away – Adam Strummers, Mark Strummers, and Brian Strummers. Next day, he finds a note on his door that says, "? Strummers. He is the one who did it!" Who threw the snowball at the man's house?

Chapter 4: Advanced Games and Teasers (Ages 13 to 15)

The advanced games and teasers provoke your mind to think more logically, especially when faced with a complex situation.[12] They require you to be fast and identify missing points easily to make something out of a situation. This chapter brings you three main types of advanced games and teasers: Read Between the Lines, Tickle Your Common Sense, and Logically Sound or Not. Answers to all the questions on this chapter can be found in chapter seven of this book.

Read Between the Lines

As the name suggests, these brain teasers are meant to help you become more attentive and smart.[13] In many cases, you have to look deeper at the information provided to get the answer.

1. A man is served tea in a restaurant. He immediately calls the waiter and says, "Waiter! There is a fly in my tea!" The waiter apologizes and says that he will return with another cup of tea. After the waiter comes back, the man takes the new cup and says, "Waiter! This is the same cup of tea!" How did he know?

---

[12] Miller, K.J., Siddarth, P., Gaines, J.M., Parrish, J., et al. (2012). The memory fitness program: Cognitive effects of a healthy aging intervention. *The American Journal of Geriatric Psychiatry, 20*(6), 514-523.

[13] Brain Den. (n.d.). Logic puzzles. Retrieved from http://brainden.com/logic-puzzles.htm

2. Some college students went camping and lit a bonfire. As they were dancing around the fire, rain started falling and put the fire out. One of the students, John, realized that he had a flashlight and eight batteries. However, four were charged while four were not. The problem is that John does not know which cells are working. How many attempts does John need to sort the charged and uncharged batteries before being able to use the flashlight?

3. There are three keys that can be used to open one door each. How many attempts do you need to know the right key for every door?

4. A gentleman is walking on the railroad. Then, he notices that the train is coming towards him. He walks towards it for some moments before stepping aside.

5. I can take you to other places that are neat. It could even be a restaurant, another country, or even a palace. I can tell you the company numbers or help you get your hotel room of choice. Policemen use me all the time when you fail to park a car appropriately. What am I?

6. I have a heart, but it never beats. I also have a home, but I never sleep there. I can take a person's house and build another. And, know what, I love playing with my brothers. Who am I?

7. When you press my button, I will always sing for you. Then, you decide my volume and song. What am I?

8. I never feel lonely because I always have six friends on my side. If my friends were not there, I would be less useful in mathematics. What am I?

Tickle Your Common Sense

These brain teasers are created to help you think harder and establish the immediate situation or operation. They are meant to take your thoughts to another level as well.

1. You are visiting your grandma who lives on the other end of the valley. Because it is her birthday, you want to carry some cakes for her.

Between your grandma's home and your house, there are seven bridges, as well as a troll that lives under every bridge that requires you to pay some toll in the form of cakes. To cross the bridges, you have to give the trolls half of the cakes you are carrying. But they are kind and give you back every cake you give. Therefore, how many cakes do you need to make so that your grandma gets two cakes?

2. Every son in John's family has as many sisters and brothers. However, every daughter has twice as many brothers as the sisters. Can you tell how many girls and boys are in John's family?

3. Your main target is to find numbers whose answer is 20. The rule is that you are only allowed to utilize 3s. For example, 3+3=6. Though you are allowed to use any function, the total has to add up to 20.

4. This is a 4-digit number that gives the same figure even when written backwards. If you add the outer digits, the figure you get is six times the sum of the two center digits. Which number is this?

5. If you dissect the number 1999 in the order 1, 9, 9, and 9, you are required to make 89. You can opt to use

brackets and common mathematical operation such as plus (+), minus (-), and even a square root (√).

6. Identify three consecutive numbers that will add to 9000.

7. James took an exam of 20 questions. Then, the exam was graded by awarding 10 points for every question that one got correct and deducting five points for every wrongly answered question. James did all the 20 questions and got a score of 125. How many questions did he get wrong?

8. James was assessing an angle that measured 14.5° using a magnifying glass. The glass magnifies the angle two times. Therefore, how large would the angle be when looked at using the glass?

Logically Sound or Not?

You may face situations that require establishing whether they are logically possible or not.[14] The following brain teasers are designed to help sharpen your brain to easily handle such circumstances.

1. A man is trapped in a room that has two doors. On the first door, there is a magnifying glass. The hot sun instantly heats up anything that enters via this door. On the second door, a fire-breathing dragon awaits. How can the man escape from the room?[15]

[14] Braingle. (2019). Brain teasers. Retrieved from https://www.braingle.com/brainteasers/All.html

[15] Bun, K.J. (2019). Karen's logic thinking puzzles: Lateral thinking riddles and brain teasers for all ages. Retrieved from

2. My little friend is called Jack. He is very lazy. When his science homework is supposed to give an answer of one pound, Jack indicates that that is too heavy. One day, he requested me to get him a pound of stuff and told me that I had three options: a) one pound of shoulder bag with holder; b) one pound of bricks with holder; and c) a stack of books weighing one pound. To give Jack the heaviest objects, what should I choose?

3. Last week, it took John three days to get from point "A" to "B." However, four days are needed to go back from point "B" to "A." Can you determine what "A" and "B" are?

4. A man left his camp and headed south for 3 miles. He then turned east and headed in that direction for 3 miles. After that, he went north for 3 miles. Eventually, he returned back to his camp and discovered a bear. What color was the bear?

5. When a doctor gives a patient three pills and asks him to take one after every 30 minutes; how long are the pills going to last?

6. There was a plumber and an electrician standing in a line for the theaters. One was the father, and the other was the son. How is this possible?

7. There was a man who stood on one side of a river. His pet dog was standing on the other side of the river. Yet, when the man called, the dog was able to run up to him without getting wet, or without using a bridge or boat. How did the dog do it?

8. The 22nd President of the United States was called Cleveland. Benjamin Harrison succeeded Cleveland to become the 23rd president of the US. However, Cleveland got back the presidency and became the 24th President. Which other US president succeeded his own successor?

9. How many letters do you get in the alphabet?

Chapter 5: Some Extras for the Daredevils!

These are complex brain teasers that are meant for kids who have managed to solve the previous brain teasers. Being smart, they need a bigger challenge! In many cases, the games can require a lot of thinking. This chapter explores the three mind teasers that are perfect for the smart ones: Radical Riddles, Grand Games, and Confusing Conundrums.

Hints are given for the most complicated brain teasers.

Radical Riddles

How about challenging the kids to word puzzles? Here are some questions that might get the kids thinking about the answers for quite a while. Put yourself to the test to sharpen your memory and hone your problem-solving skills.[16]

1. I can speak, but I do not have a mouth. I can hear, but I do not have ears. I do not have a body, but you will get me alive with the wind. What exactly am I? (Hint: The riddle tricks you into thinking about mouth and ears.)

2. When you measure his life, he expires. He is quick when thin but slow when fat. His biggest enemy is wind. (Hint: What threatens the wind more than anything?)

---

[16] Pennington, M. (n.d.). 25 of the hardest riddles ever. Can you solve them? Retrieved from https://www.rd.com/funny-stuff/challenging-riddles/

3. It has cities, but they are void of houses. It also has mountains but is devoid of trees. It has water, but it lacks fish. What exactly is it? (Hint: You better think of something inanimate.)

4. What do you see in mid-March and April but not at the start or end of either of the months? (Hint: Be literal.)

5. You notice a boat that is carrying people across the water. It is floating in the sea and has not sunk. However, when you check again, you do not see a single person. Why?[17] (Hint: Think about the "single" word.)

6. What English word is discussed in the following details?

    (a) The first two letters are used to signify a male.

    (b) The first three letters are used to signify a female.

    (c) The first four letters are used to signify a great

    (d) The whole word is used to signify a woman.
        (Hint: Identify a word that holds all the others.)

7. Identify a word that features three consecutive double letters. (Hint: The first letter and the last letters will form a set of double letters when combined).

8. Can you name a five-letter word that becomes shorter when you add two letters to it? (Hint: The answer is in the question!)

9. It comes from a mine and is then surrounded by woods. Everyone uses it. What is it? (Hint: Consider the wood detail.)

---

[17] Williams, B. (2019). *Amazing brain teasers: Mind-blowing logic and math challenges.* Chicago: Prodinnova.

10. What disappears immediately after being named? (Hint: Focus on conceptual metaphor.)[18]

11. Is it possible for four to be half of five? (Hint: Think literally.)

12. It has keys but lacks a lock, space, and room. You can enter, but it is impossible to get outside. What is it? (Hint: Think about the word "key".)

Confusing Conundrums

These brain teasers are created to sound confusing. However, with just a little bit of thought, kids may be able to find the answer! Plus, the look on their faces when they solve the riddle is priceless. Even if you thought you had mastered the previous mind teasers, you might still find the below questions rather challenging.

1. "A" is a brother to "B," who is the brother of "C." "C" is a dad to "D." From this information, how is "A" related to "D"? (Hint: Follow logic to get it right).

2. Using the combination provided, can you identify the next three letters for OTTFFSS?[19] (Hint: Though these letters appear random, they have a pattern. Take a closer look at the common strings of words).

3. Though this belongs to you, it is genuinely used by all people.

4. First, conceptualize the colors of clouds in the sky, the snow, and the bright moon. Now, what do cows drink?

[18] Foster, H. (2019). *Riddles, brain teasers, and trick questions for kids: A fun book of questions for you and your friends!* New York: Willy & Sons.

[19] Nowak, C. (n.d.). 19 brain teasers that will leave you stumped. Retrieved from https://www.rd.com/culture/brain-teasers/

(Hint: Though this riddle is not complex, it takes your mind through a long journey to confuse you. Now, you need to deviate from it to get the answer.)

5. If you look at the numbers from one to 10, can you establish how seven is different? (Hint: Think simply.)

6. Everything starts with you eating me. Then, you will also be eaten. What exactly am I? (Hint: Keep it simple.)

7. It comes once every minute, only twice in a moment, but it will never come in 1000 years. (Hint: Although invoking numbers might look an easier option, consider looking away from numbers to get the right answer.)

8. A lady pushes her car to a hotel and informs the hotel manager that she is bankrupt. Why?

9. You are looking at a photo of someone in an album. Then, your friend asks, "Who is it?" You reply, "Sisters and brothers, I have none. But that man's dad is my father's son." Who are you looking at in the photo?

10. John left his home running. He looked left, ran the same distance, and looked left again. After running a similar distance, he turned left once more. When he finally returned home, he met two masked men. Can you name the masked men?

Grand Games

Finally, here are some apps that you can use to test your logic skills. Not only do these apps provide some serious challenges for the kids, but they can keep them entertained for hours. Additionally, you can set the difficulty levels in the applications, letting the kids start at an easy level and increase the difficulty as they get better at the games.

It is also important to engage in several games to sharpen the brain more effectively. Here are the three top games you should consider.

1. Lumosity

This is one of the leading brain teasers in the market today. It can be used as an app for either mobile phone or PC.[20] The good thing about Lumosity is that you can customize it to different complexity levels.

The game is designed with the latest artificial intelligence (AI) applications so that it can understand and knows you over time. It operates with different parts of the brain to allow you to easily pick what to work with and for how long.

Lumosity helps to simplify science so that you can exercise your brain and sharpen your skills every day. Whether you want to enhance your personal ability to concentrate or increase flexibility, this is one grand game you should consider.[21]

The only shortcoming of the game is that it comes at a cost. After the trial period is over, you are required to upgrade to the paid version.

---

[20] Lumosity. (n.d.). Retrieved from https://www.lumosity.com/en/

[21] Major, C. (2016). 17 best brain training games for Android. Retrieved from https://www.developinghumanbrain.org/brain-training-games-android/

2. Brain Café

This is another leading game in the market that is designed to teach you about geography and planet. It is created with thousands of questions that help to demonstrate how its systems work.

Like Lumosity, you can use Brain Café to select the preferred level of game difficulty to develop your skills progressively. Note that you can play it regardless of your age. Simply customize the game to match your requirements.

Brain Café provides a unique level of interaction so that you can feel part of the environment and get the anticipated satisfaction. However, it does involve paid feature.

3. Happify

This is another grand game that will help you to stay positive in life. The game is very effective in helping you sharpen your memory and remain productive (useful for kids who might need a little boost during classes).[22]

The first thing that determines whether you will succeed in life is your perception. This game helps you to feel good and take control over your happiness. Besides, it also helps

---

[22] Spicer, J. & Sanborn, A. (2019). What does the mind learn? *A comparison of human and machine learning representations.* Current Opinion in Neurobiology, 55, 97-102.

you to overcome stress and stay focused on things you consider important in life.

Do not simply engage in any activity out there; look for the options that have been proven to work in sharpening the mind. Remember that you can also use Happify to measure your happiness score.

Chapter 6: Brain Teaser Trivia

When you answer a brain teaser correctly, one question that might run through your mind is: "How can you become a leading scorer in top teaser trivia?" Most of the people you see scoring top marks in different brain teasers and puzzles have taken a lot of time to study and understand how they work. In this chapter, we will look at geniuses in brain-teasing and provide you with useful tips on becoming a pro in brain teasers.

Do You Know These Geniuses?

1. Thomas Snyder: Snyder is an American brain teasing genius who has made a name for setting the world record of solving a complex Sudoku in only one minute 23.93 seconds.[23] He was a worker at Stanford University where he specialized in biomechanics. His venture into science made him explore brain teasers as science. He was also very persistent in exploring different levels of brain teasers.

2. Kota Morinishi: Like Snyder, Morinishi was another Sudoku enthusiast who won the Japanese Sudoku challenge of 2014. He likes to keep his mind sharp with mind-boggling teasers. He is an architect graduate

---

[23] Sudoku.com. (n.d.). Sudoku lessons from world champion Thomas Snyder. Retrieved from https://sudoku.com/how-to-play/sudoku-lessons-from-world-champion-thomas-snyder/

from the University of Tokyo and emphasizes that brain teasers are a personal hobby.[24]

3. Jan Mrozowski: Mrozowski is a polish national who won the Sudoku competition in 2010. He won the competition that involved solving 10 puzzles. He took 54 minutes to solve them.

The most notable thing about Mrozowski is his persistence on brain teasers. Like the other two geniuses, Morinishi and Snyder, Mrozowski indicated that he takes brain teasers as a daily challenge to keep his mind sharp all the time.

How To Be a Brain Teaser Pro

If you take a closer look at the pros in brain teasers, the one thing that they have in common is persistence. They are always looking for the next challenge that can help to grow their minds. Now, you do not have to simply read about the geniuses in books; you can also become a brain teaser pro by following these tricks:

Be Methodical

Working on brain teasers requires that you take a methodical approach. This means crafting routines that you can follow to solve different teasers. For example, you

---

[24] International Business Times. (2014). Kota Morinishi is first Japanese Sudoku champion. Retrieved from https://www.ibtimes.co.uk/kota-morinishi-first-japanese-sudoku-champion-1461485

can use the elimination method to tick out the odd options and increase the chances of getting the right answer.

Develop an Interest in Brain Teasers

You can only become a pro if you are interested in brain teasers. This will motivate you to keep exploring new and more complex challenges. It is advisable to practice with brain teasers on a daily basis.

Learn From the Geniuses

When you read about the pros who have won different brain teaser challenges in the globe, they can provide a lot of motivation. Some have demonstrated that they have developed an interest in teasers so much that it is like a hobby to them. Therefore, if you can follow the footsteps of these experts, you will also become an expert.

Always Remain Calm and Get the Right Environment

To become a pro, it is important to ensure that you only work on brain teasers in the right environment. The target is ensuring you have total concentration and solving the teasers correctly.

Mystify Your Friends

After exploring different levels of mind teasers, it is time to get your friends to appreciate your advancement. It will give you the motivation to keep exploring additional levels. You could also learn from other mind teaser enthusiasts in your social circles. Here are three ways to mystify your friends:

1. Challenge them to participate in a brain-teasing competition

One way of showing how pro you are is getting down with what you love; solving brain teasers. When your friends join the challenge, you can use your brain-teasing skills to get answers at lightning speed and knock them off.

2. Tell them to come and witness major challenges

Another way of mystifying your friends is asking them to come and witness when you are competing with other pros. Whether at the local or international level, they will be left with one question in their minds: "How did you do it?"

3. Start teaching others how to solve brain teasers

One way of standing out and making close friends come running to you is acting like a pro. You can demonstrate this by starting a brain-teasing class online to help those who are interested in brain teasers. This will also help you to continue sharpening your mind.

Conclusion

Brain teasers can play a crucial part in a child's cognitive development. When used at different stages of personal growth, it has been said that brain games can help to sharpen the brain, promote memory, and potentially reduce degenerative conditions of the brain.

To get more from the brain teasers, it is prudent to take the challenge progressively and move towards the more complex brain teasers over time. For young children, it is advisable to start with the simple wordplay that makes mind-teasing fun. Then, the challenge should be advanced to more complex arithmetic activities and mind-boggling mysteries.

At advanced levels, you can consider going for complex brain teasers that require holistic thinking to get the answers. You can also become one of the experts in mind teasers and enjoy the revered status whether at competition levels or among your friends.

Whether you want to use brain teasers for fun or for competitions, it is prudent to be consistent. You need to make it part of you and explore different types of teasers to sharpen the mind.

Do not keep wondering about the best ways to sharpen your mind: use brain teasers!

Don't forget,
if you like my book,
or even if you don't,
I want to hear about it!
I encouraged you to leave
A review on Amazon.
Help others decide to buy!

The Answers!

This chapter is a presentation of answers to all the brain teasers in this book.

Fun Wordplay
1. Baby, Body
2. These are some of the words you can make:
    - 2 letter words: bo, lo, oh, so, us
    - 3 letter words: boo, bus, cob, cub, hob, lob, loo (this might get a laugh or two), ooh, sub
    - 4 letter words: boss, bush, club, cobs, cool, cubs, lobs, loss, lush, shoo, solo, such
    - 5 letter words: blush, clubs, cools, shool, slush, solos
    - 6 letter words: school, slouch
3. airplane
4. Plate
5. The Letter "M"
6. Age

Brain Benders
1. Home alone
2. Repeat after Me
3. Breaking the rules
4. Calculated risk
5. Upper class, high class
6. The odd against us
7. Left brain
8. Irregular heartbeat
9. Doctor in the house
10. Mixed nuts

Quick Questionnaire

1. Stairs
2. Map
3. Chalkboard
4. Shorter
5. Clock
6. Hole
7. Stamp
8. Piano
9. Sponge
10. Towel

Arithmetic Activities

1. They bought a total of three tickets because the granddad is also a dad, and the dad is also a son.
2. You can have three answers for this question. The father could be 51 years old and the son 15 years old, the father 42 and the son 24 years old or the father 60 and the son 06 years old.
3. $18 (about $4.5 per leg)
4. The number Seven. If you remove the letter "S", it becomes "Even."
5. 9 tomatoes
6. $15.50
7. Neither. They both weigh the same!
8. 16 tables
9. Jane
10. Zero (Reason: Roosters do not lay eggs.)

Puzzling Puzzles

1. Greenhouses are made of glass!

2. Since the tools you have are random, you only need to pour water into the pipe, and the ball will float up to the surface.

3. When you throw a ball up into the sky, it is stopped by gravity and starts falling back to the surface.

4. To know the rod that is a magnet, consider hanging the rods on a string and see the one that turns to face the true north. You can also take one rod and touch the other in the middle. If the metals get closer to each other, you are holding a magnet.

5. The eldest son. You do not need to mow the lawn during snow!

6. Clocks can measure time when not showing it correctly. To know the right time, you only need to wind the clock up. Here, it is important to assume that the trip to the friend and back took the same time. Besides, it is also important to assume that the friend also has a clock that showed the right time.

7. In this question, there are two possible answers. Solution 1: If angels "C" and "B" have the aura of the same color, then, the chances are that angel "A" must have shouted his color. Then, others followed by saying about theirs too. Solution 2: If angels "C" and "B" had different colors, angel "A" must have remained silent, which would be a sign for angel "B" who could easily tell (by looking at angle "C") what his color was.

8. Though there are many possible reasons for this, the chances are that the lady is of short stature. Because she cannot reach the upper section of the elevator, she can ask other people in the elevator to push it for

her. On the rainy days, she can use the umbrella to push the buttons. In other cases, she only alights on the 7th floor because she can reach the seventh button only.

9. It is a one storey house! It does not have any stairs.

Mind-Boggling Mysteries

1. As there is more than one clock in the room, each clock is displaying a different time.
2. The man's horse was named Sunday!
3. Simple, the man has to light the match first!
4. Pages 15 and 16 are printed back-to-back. Which means, there is no place to keep a ten dollar note!
5. Mark said to Jack that he stopped imagining and therefore, escaped the room!
6. The man was bald.
7. The note says "? Strummers" which means "Question MARK Strummers." Mark was the one who threw the snowball.
8. The wife and sister are Siamese twins.
9. He noticed the bird at about 20,000 feet getting sucked into the engine.
10. The man's work is in a lighthouse. Therefore, by turning on the light, he killed a dozen of hundred people. After reading about it in the newspaper in the morning, he kills himself.

Read Between the Lines

1. He has spooned in sugar in his tea before giving it away to the waiter. Now isn't that smart?!
2. John needs to sort the batteries into three main groups. Two groups should have three batteries and

the last one should have two. This will guarantee John that he at least have two working batteries. For the groups that have three batteries, John will need three attempts to establish if two batteries in the group are charged (battery 1+battery 2, battery 2+battery 3, and battery 1 + battery 3.) For the group of battery that has two batteries, he will only need one attempt. Therefore, the total attempts will be 1+3+3=7.

3. The answer is 6 attempts. For key one, you will need three attempts for all the doors. For key two, you will need two attempts for the remaining two doors, and the last key will only be tested on one last door.

4. The man was on the railway bridge and had to move some distance to step aside from the railroad.

5. The answer is a book. Novels help you to explore new places, countries and even palaces. You can also book a restaurant, book a meal or a boarding room. For a criminal and people who park wrongly in the city, the police can also book them in.

6. The answer is the king of hearts in your deck of playing cards.

7. The answer is a CD player.

8. The answer is a dice cube. It is made of 6 sides and its friends are all the six numbers on each side.

Tickle Your Common Sense

1. You need only two cakes. This is because every time you give the trolls your cake, they give it back.

2. The answer is that there are three girls and four boys in the family (every boy has 3 sisters and 3 brothers, however, every girl has 2 sisters and 4 brothers)

3. The first part is a fraction, 3(fraction). This implies that 3x2x1=6. Then, you should divide by three to get the answer. The sum will be 20.
4. The number is 6116. Whether you write it from front or backwards, it gives the same figure. If you add the outer digits (6+6=12) the answer is six times the sum of inner digits (1+1=2).
5. (5) The answer is 89=-1+9(9*9)
6. 2999,3000,3001
7. John answered five questions wrongly. If he had gotten right all the questions, the total score would have been 200. Because he managed 125, it implies that he lost 75 points. The 75 points are divided by 15 (10 points for the questions he did not get right and 5 points deducted for not getting it right).
8. The angle would still appear 14.2 degrees.

Logically Sound or Not?
1. The man has to simply wait for the night time in order to get out when there is no sunlight.
2. The heaviest object should be a box holding the bricks. Because it is made of thick wooden material, the total load will weigh more. Note that every object other than the holder weighs the same; one pound.
3. "A" and "B" are days of the week, Sunday and Wednesday.
4. The only point on Earth where you can go 3 miles south, 3 miles east, and then 3 miles north to go back to your first position is the North Pole. By this, we can say that the bear is white.
5. The pills will last for only one hour. The patient will take one pill immediately, another after 30 minutes, and the last after another 30 minutes.

6. They were a couple; a husband and wife.
7. The river was frozen.
8. Benjamin Harrison. He took power from Cleveland who was also his successor.
9. Eleven. You might be tempted to think that the answer is 26. Good trial but only if you are talking about English alphabets. Take a closer look and you will realize that the answer is 11 letters.

Radical Riddles
1. Echo
2. Candle
3. A map
4. The answer is the letter "R."
5. All the people were married.
6. Heroine
7. Bookkeeper
8. The word is "short"!
9. The pencil lead
10. Silence
11. IV, the Roman numeral used to denote 4, is half (two letters) of those used to denote 5.
12. A Keyboard

Confusing Conundrums
1. "D" is an aunt to "A."
2. The answer is E N T. Every letter denotes the first letters of numbers one to five (1, 2, 3, 4, 5, ...)
3. The answer is your "name."
4. The answer is water.
5. Seven has two syllables while the others have only one.
6. Fish hook

7. Letter "M"
8. The lady is playing monopoly.
9. Your son
10. The umpire and catcher

References

Argasinski, J. & Wegrzyn, P. (2018). Affective patterns in serious games. *Future Generation Computer Systems, 92*, 526-538. doi: 10.1016/j.future.2018.06.013

Bar-Hillel, M. & Ruma, F. (1982). Some teasers concerning conditional probabilities. *Cognition, 11*(2), 109–122.

Brain Den. (n.d.). Logic puzzles. Retrieved from http://brainden.com/logic-puzzles.htm

Braingle. (2019). Brain teasers. Retrieved from https://www.braingle.com/brainteasers/All.html

Bun, K.J. (2019). Karen's logic thinking puzzles: Lateral thinking riddles and brain teasers for all ages. Retrieved from https://www.goodreads.com/book/show/44047168-karen-s-logic-thinking-puzzles

Dashner, J. (2008). The journal of curious letters. Washington: Shadow Mountain.

Foster, H. (2019). *Riddles, brain teasers, and trick questions for kids: A fun book of questions for you and your friends!* New York: Willy & Sons.

Gardner, M. (1954). *The second scientific American book of mathematical puzzles and diversions.* New York: Simon & Schuster.

Happify. (n.d.). Retrieved from https://www.happify.com/

International Business Times. (2014). Kota Morinishi is first Japanese Sudoku champion. Retrieved from https://www.ibtimes.co.uk/kota-morinishi-first-japanese-sudoku-champion-1461485

Lumosity. (n.d.). Retrieved from https://www.lumosity.com/en/

Major, C. (2016). 17 best brain training games for Android. Retrieved from https://www.developinghumanbrain.org/brain-training-games-android/

Miller, K.J., Siddarth, P., Gaines, J.M., Parrish, J., et al. (2012). The memory fitness program: Cognitive effects of a healthy aging intervention. *The American Journal of Geriatric Psychiatry, 20*(6), 514-523.

Moore, G. (2010). *10-minute brain teasers: Brain-training tips, logic tests, and puzzles to exercise your mind.* New York: Skyhorse.

Nowak, C. (n.d.). 19 brain teasers that will leave you stumped. Retrieved from https://www.rd.com/culture/brain-teasers/

Pennington, M. (n.d.). 25 of the hardest riddles ever. Can you solve them? Retrieved from https://www.rd.com/funny-stuff/challenging-riddles/

Price, M. (2017). John Hopkins Researchers say doing this will improve your brain power. Retrieved from http://fortune.com/2017/10/23/johns-hopkins-brain-function/

Reader's Digest Association. (2007). *Puzzles & brain teasers: Sudoku puzzles, word games, visual challenges, and tests of logic.* Washington: Reader's Digest Association.

Reader's Digest. (2004). *Reader's Digest book of puzzles & brain teasers.* New York: Reader's Digest Association.

Realizations Inc. (n.d.). Set fifty-six. Retrieved from https://arlenetaylor.org/brain-exercises/brain-benders/549-set-fifty-six

Riddles. (2017). Math riddles. Retrieved from https://www.getriddles.com/math-riddles/

Silverthorne, S. & Warner, J. (2010). *Mind-boggling one-minute mysteries and brain teasers*. New York: Harvest House.

Spicer, J. & Sanborn, A. (2019). What does the mind learn? A comparison of human and machine learning representations. *Current Opinion in Neurobiology, 55*, 97-102.

Sudoku.com. (n.d.). Sudoku lessons from world champion Thomas Snyder. Retrieved from https://sudoku.com/how-to-play/sudoku-lessons-from-world-champion-thomas-snyder/

Vervoort, J. (2019). New frontiers in futures games: leveraging game sector developments. *Futures, 105*, 174-186.

Williams, B. (2019). *Amazing brain teasers: Mind-blowing logic and math challenges*. Chicago: Prodinnova.

Made in the USA
Middletown, DE
11 July 2019